Miss Brooks Loves Books!

(and I don't)

STORY BY

Barbara Bottner

ILLUSTRATIONS BY

Michael Emberley

Dragonfly Books · New York

For William Steig, who started it all.
—B.B.

For super teacher Deb Marciano,
#1 fan of books, kids, and authors,
and mentor for the next generation of super teachers.
—M.E.

Text copyright © 2010 by Barbara Bottner
Illustrations copyright © 2010 by Bird Productions, Inc.

All rights reserved. Published in the United States by Dragonfly Books, an imprint of
Random House Children's Books, a division of Penguin Random House LLC, New York.
Originally published in hardcover in the United States by Alfred A. Knopf Books for Young Readers,
an imprint of Random House Children's Books, a division of Penguin Random House LLC, New York, in 2010.

Dragonfly Books and the colophon are registered trademarks of Penguin Random House LLC.

Visit us on the Web! rhcbooks.com

Educators and librarians, for a variety of teaching tools, visit us at RHTeachersLibrarians.com

The Library of Congress has cataloged the hardcover edition of this work as follows:
Bottner, Barbara.
Miss Brooks loves books! (and I don't) / by Barbara Bottner ; illustrations by Michael Emberley. — 1st ed.
p. cm.
Summary: A first-grade girl who does not like to read stubbornly resists her school librarian's efforts
to convince her to love books until she finds one that might change her mind.
ISBN 978-0-375-84682-3 (trade) — ISBN 978-0-375-94682-0 (lib. bdg.) — ISBN 978-0-307-75945-0 (ebook)
[1. Books and reading—Fiction. 2. Librarians—Fiction. 3. Schools—Fiction. 4. Steig, William, 1907–2003.
Shrek!] I. Emberley, Michael, ill. II. Title. III. Title: Miss Brooks loves books! (and I do not).
PZ7.B6586Mi 2010
[E]—dc22
2009002305

ISBN 978-1-9848-5210-6 (pbk.)

MANUFACTURED IN CHINA
10 9 8 7 6 5 4 3 2
First Dragonfly Books Edition

Miss Brooks is our librarian. She loves books. A lot.

She loves *The Runaway Bunny*.
And *Babar*. And *Where the Wild Things
Are*. And *The Very Hungry Caterpillar*.

I ask Miss Brooks why she dresses up for reading circle.

"I want you to get as excited about books as I am," she says.

I think Miss Brooks gets a little too excited. And I bet her costumes itch.

Halloween means we each have to find a poem
to share. But all the books with witches, ghosts,
and goblins are checked out. And I hate pumpkins.

So I make up a Halloween poem of my own.

The class looks at me funny. Miss Brooks says, "Well, it's a start."

All year long, Miss Brooks reads us
books. Books about dragons and Pilgrims
and presidents. Books about love and
leprechauns. Groundhogs, even!
It's vexing.

Then, in May, Miss Brooks tells us about something truly terrifying: *Book Week!*

"You each need to pick a favorite story to share with the class. I want you to wear a costume and tell us all about it. Really show us why you love it!" she says.

IT'S BOOK WEEK!!

"I'll never love a book the way you do," I tell Miss Brooks.
"Don't be so sure," she says.

When I get home, I ask my mother if we can move to a new town. My mother says there's a librarian in every town.

I ask if she wants to do my assignment for me.
"I've already been in the first grade," says my mother.

Every single day of Book Week, kids share stories about trains and fairies and cowboys and dogs.

When Miss Brooks asks what I think, I say,

"Too flowery."

"Too furry."

"Too clickety."

"Too yippity."

So Miss Brooks fills my bag with more books for me to read with my mom.

But I don't like any of them. "They're too kissy. Too pink. And too silly," I tell my mother.

"You're as stubborn as a wart," she says.

Warts?

"I want to read a story with warts!" I shout.

My mother finds a book called *Shrek!* Shrek has hairs on his nose. And he snorts. I love that!

"Can you read it again?" I ask.

I love this book!

I have to practice the words over and over, but my mother helps. Then we make an ogre costume. I make stick-on warts for the whole class.

When I get to school the next day, I ask Miss Brooks
to lend me a hand.

When I say the word "snort," the whole class snorts.
I explain why a stubborn, smelly, snorty ogre, searching
for a revolting bride, makes me laugh.

Miss Brooks says she's glad I found a book to love.

She says that even ogres (like me) can find something funny and fantastic and appalling in the library.

And that is the slimy truth.